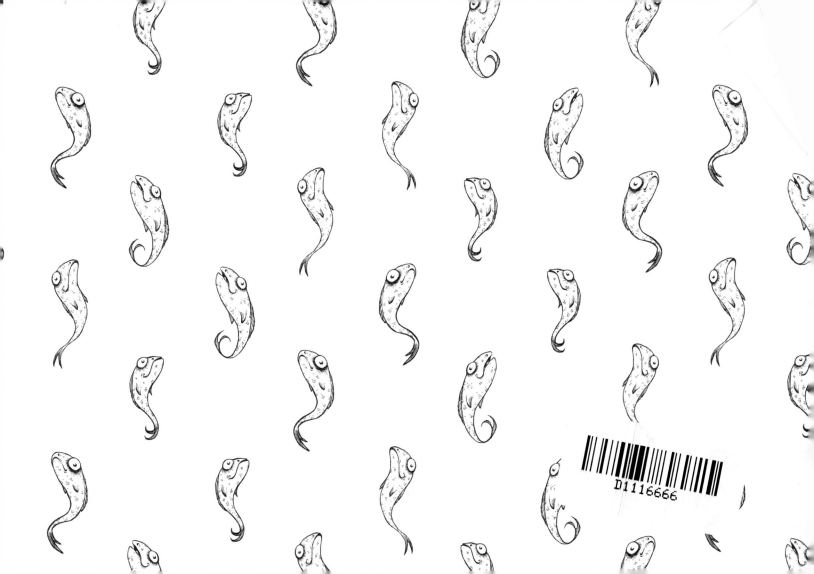

D1116666

James Joyce

THE CATS OF COPENHAGEN

SCRIBNER

New York London Toronto Sydney New Delhi

Preface

Exquisite, minuscule, and with a strong, almost anarchic subtext, *The Cats of Copenhagen* is a slightly younger twin sister to *The Cat and the Devil,* the only other known example of James Joyce writing a story for young children. Both works, written within a few weeks of each other, are in letters posted to Stephen James Joyce, his only grandchild. Clearly, cats were a common currency between them: cats, and their common need to have somebody around to help them cross the road.

When he wrote to his grandson on August 10, 1936, telling him about the cat and the devil of Beaugency (he was writing from Villiers-sur-Mer in Calvados), Joyce let him know that a few days earlier he had sent on for him "a little cat filled with sweets"—a kind of Trojan cat to outwit the grown-ups. Another great idea pinched from Homer!

Like many otherwise sensible people, James Joyce detested, even loathed, dogs; but he thought the world of cats. In the first chapter of *Ulysses* in which Leopold Bloom appears, the very first conversation is between a hungry feline and kind-hearted Bloom:

—Mkgnao!
—O, there you are, Mr. Bloom said, turning from the fire.
The cat mewed in answer and stalked again stiffly round a leg of the table, mewing.

No one had read this delightful little story (*The Cats,* not *Ulysses*!) for a very long time and, indeed, it was almost entirely lost and forgotten. It is a joy to see it appear for the first time ever in print in the United States.

A Brief History

In March 2006, Hans E. Jahnke generously donated a battered trunkful of miscellaneous material to the Zurich James Joyce Foundation, where the leonine Fritz Senn is director. Hans is the stepson of James Joyce's son George (Giorgio). He inherited these important papers from his mother, Asta, Giorgio's second wife. Among many items of great interest are the letters sent by Joyce to Helen Fleischman, Giorgio's first wife and Stephen's mother. Included is one he penned specially for little Stephen, four years of age, recounting a brief and entertaining children's story, *The Cats of Copenhagen*.

An intimate and enduring relationship had formed between grandfather and grandson, on the occasion of whose birth on February 15, 1932 (not long after the loss of the author's own larger-than-life father), James Joyce composed perhaps his most tender poem, *Ecce Puer*.

> *Young life is breathed*
> *On the glass;*
> *The world that was not*
> *Come to pass*
>
> (3rd verse)

As *The Cats of Copenhagen* letter (presumably posted in a red letterbox in Copenhagen) is dated September 5, 1936, we can place it in context with his current travels and plans.

Stephen was staying at the Villa des Roses in Menthon-Saint-Bernard, and Joyce was taking a break in Denmark. The writer's finances were precarious; his commitments were complicated and worrisome; and the idea of escaping Paris to the relative oasis of Copenhagen appealed to him. He spoke passable Danish and liked to say that, in common with other Dubliners of Viking ancestry, good Danish blood ran in his veins. The Copenhagen

Interlude, he felt, would afford him the much-needed opportunity to relax over a glass of wine ("*at bastille en flaske vin*") and also get some work done ("*ar bastille noget*"). And while there in Hamlet's homeland he could push on the business of a Danish edition of *Ulysses* (not finally realized until 1949, in translation by Morgens Boisen). Lastly, any spare time could be devoted to reading over proofs for the long-awaited Bodley Head edition of *Ulysses,* the first English edition to be actually printed in England.

As it turned out, his sojourn in Denmark was a great success. He especially liked the letterboxes, and the redcoated postmen put him in mind of Shaun, dogged postman of *Finnegans Wake.* He planned to go back to Copenhagen the next spring and rent a place. He liked the Danes, a "nation of weepers" and a race of "wild men with soft voices," as he put it, quite like the Irish. Dublin, of course, was founded one thousand years ago by Danes. And he used lots of Danish in drafting his then work in progress, *Finnegans Wake.*

Alas, unlike Finnegan, he was never to return; or so the biographers tell us. The only way to *really* find out would be to go there ourselves and see if he ever did manage to sneak in *Cats.*

THE CATS
OF COPENHAGEN

ALAS I cannot send you a Copenhagen cat

because there are NO cATS in CopenHageN.

There are **LOTS** & **LOTS** of *FISH*

and **BICYCLE** but

there are **NO CATS.**

Also there are no **POLICEMEN.**

ALL THE
Danish
policemen
pass the
DAY AT HOME
in bed.

They smoke BIG DaNiSH cigaRs

and drink buttermilk

all day lOnG.

There are lots and lots of young boys

dressed in red on bicycles

going around all da**y**

with **telegrams**

and letters

and POSTCARDS.

These are all for the **policemen**

from **old Ladies** who want to cross the road

and boys who are writing home

for more **SWEETS**

and girls who want to know
something about the moon.

The policemen read them all in bed,

SMOKING all the time

and drinking *buttermilk.*

And then they give their orders

and the RED BOYS

go back and tell everybody

just what to do.

When I come to **Copenhagen** again

I will bring a ℰ𝒜𝒯 and show

the 𝔇𝔞𝔫𝔢𝔰 how it can cross the road

without any **INSTRUCTIONS**

from a ℙᴏʟɪᴄᴇᴍᴀɴ

and it will be much cheaper

(think of that!)

for a **cat**

to show them

WHAT TO DO.

Just fancy a cat **staying in bed**

all day

smoking cigars!

And as for **buttermilk!**

No **CAT**

would drink it at all.

And t*h*en there is

such a LOT of *fish*

for them.

WHAT

do

you

think

of

this

?

About the Author

James Joyce was born on February 2, 1882, in Dublin, Ireland. His subtle yet frank portrayal of human nature, coupled with his mastery of language, made him one of the most influential novelists of the twentieth century. Joyce is best known for his experimental use of language and his exploration of new literary methods. His use of the "stream-of-consciousness" literary technique reveals the flow of impressions, half thoughts, associations, hesitations, impulses, and rational thoughts of his characters. The main strength of his masterpiece novel, *Ulysses* (1922), lies in the depth of character portrayed using this technique. Joyce's other major works include *Dubliners* (1914), a collection of short stories that portray his native city; a semi-autobiographical novel called *A Portrait of the Artist as a Young Man* (1916); and *Finnegans Wake* (1939), an experimental novel that first appeared in the form of extracts from 1928 to 1937 as *Work in Progress*. He died in 1941.

About the Illustrator

Casey Sorrow is a cartoonist, printmaker, and illustrator. He was classically trained and raised on a steady diet of *The Muppets,* Schulz's *Peanuts,* and Kung Fu movies. A rebellious streak and a quick, quirky humor underpin his artwork and its focus on pop-culture iconography. Casey derives much of his inspiration from his father's lauded military service and from the war imagery of vintage comics. He lives and works in Michigan, "America's High Five."

SCRIBNER
A Division of Simon & Schuster, Inc.
1230 Avenue of the Americas
New York, NY 10020

This book is a work of fiction. Names, characters, places,
and incidents either are products of the author's imagination
or are used fictitiously. Any resemblance to actual events
or locales or persons, living or dead, is entirely coincidental.

First Scribner hardcover edition October 2012

SCRIBNER and design are registered trademarks
of The Gale Group, Inc., used under license by
Simon & Schuster, Inc., the publisher of this work.

For information about special discounts for bulk purchases,
please contact Simon & Schuster Special Sales at 1-866-506-1949
or business@simonandschuster.com.

The Simon & Schuster Speakers Bureau can bring authors to
your live event. For more information or to book an event contact
the Simon & Schuster Speakers Bureau at 1-866-248-3049
or visit our website at www.simonspeakers.com.

Manufactured in the United States of America

10 9 8 7 6 5 4 3 2 1

Library of Congress Control Number: 2012028414

ISBN 978-1-4767-0894-2
ISBN 978-1-4767-0895-9 (ebook)

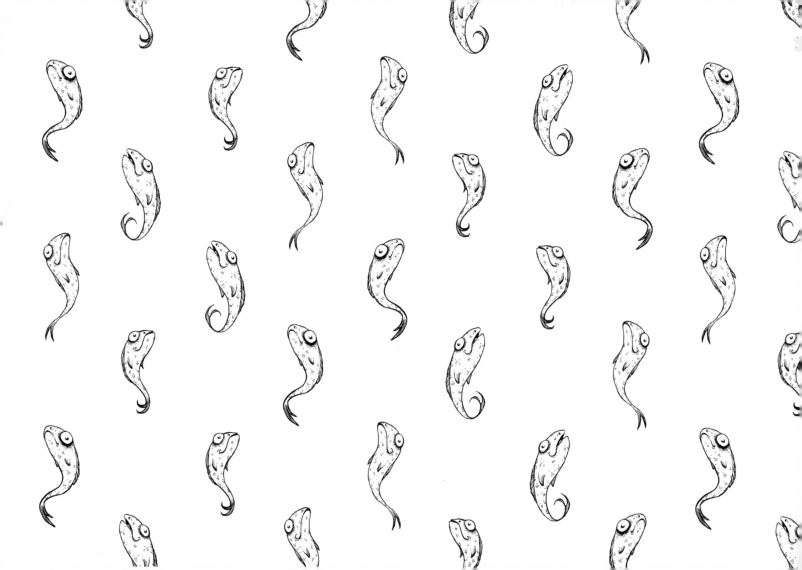